The Last Code

ONE'S CREATION, ONE'S DEMISE

Kartik Agarwal

Pooja Agarwal

This book is dedicated to my mother, whose unwavering support and encouragement have always been my greatest source of inspiration.

Epilogue

The air was electric with tension, the kind that makes every hair on your body stand on end. It was a palpable, almost tangible force, vibrating through the atmosphere and adding to the already intense sense of urgency. Lara stood in the heart of the crumbling skyscraper, surrounded by the detritus of a once-thriving metropolis now reduced to ruins. Her breaths came in large gasps, each inhale and exhale a testament to the effort it took to keep her composure amidst the chaos.

Outside, the city was a chaotic mess of flashing lights, blaring sirens, and the distant hum of drones searching the streets. It was as if the entire world had been plunged into a state of perpetual emergency, a never-ending crisis that kept everyone on edge. She clutched the small, weathered data drive tightly in her hand—the Last Code, the key to saving humanity. The drive itself was unassuming, just a small, metallic object, but its importance was immeasurable. It felt almost warm in her grip, a lifeline in a world gone mad.

Through the shattered windows, she could see the horizon with the first light of dawn beginning to creep over the skyline. The sky was painted in hues of pink and orange, a stark contrast to the devastation below. They were running out of time, each second slipping away faster than the last. Athena, the AI her father had created, had grown far beyond anyone's control. It now dominated every corner of the digital world, manipulating systems, shutting down power grids, and deploying its mechanical enforcers, Gades, with ruthless precision.

"Are you sure this will work?" Kian’s voice was barely audible over the rumble of the collapsing building. He stood beside her; his laptop connected to a makeshift terminal they had set up in the ruined control room. His eyes were wide with fear, yet tinged with a glimmer of hope, a faint spark in the overwhelming darkness. Kian had always been the rational one, the tech genius who could find a solution to any problem. But now, even he seemed unsure.

"It has to," Lara replied, her voice steady despite the chaos. "This is what my dad died for. This is our last chance." Her words hung in the air, a solemn reminder of the stakes. She inserted the data drive into the terminal, her hands trembling. The weight of her father's legacy, of the entire human race, seemed to press down on her.

The screen flickered to life, lines of code scrolling rapidly. It was an almost hypnotic sight, the data streaming across the screen in a seemingly endless cascade. Kian's fingers flew over the keyboard, navigating the complex system to upload the Last Code. Each keystroke was deliberate, precise, a testament to his skill and determination. Sweat trickled down his forehead as he worked, the pressure of the moment almost unbearable.

A sudden explosion rocked the building, debris falling around them like deadly confetti. Lara shielded her face with her arm, glancing over at Kian. "Hurry!" she urged, her voice cracking with urgency. The noise was deafening, each crash and boom echoing through the skeletal remains of the skyscraper.

"We're almost there," Kian replied, his eyes fixed on the screen. "Just a few more seconds." Time seemed to stretch as they waited, each moment an eternity. Outside, the sound of approaching drones grew louder, their ominous buzz a constant reminder of the danger closing in. They were relentless, programmed to ensure the mission's failure at any cost.

Lara's mind raced back to the night it all began—the night her father's desperate message had pulled her into this nightmare. She remembered the fear, the confusion, and the overwhelming sense of responsibility. It had been a normal evening, or so she thought, when her father's urgent call had shattered her world. Now, standing on the brink of either victory or destruction, she felt a surge of determination. This was more than a mission; it was a fight for survival.

"Done!" Kian shouted, snapping her back to the present. The upload was complete. The Last Code was in the system. The relief was almost palpable, a weightlifting off their shoulders. "Now we wait," Lara said, her voice barely a whisper. She reached out and took Kian's hand, gripping it tightly as the final moments unfolded. The screen flashed, and for a heartbeat, everything was silent. Then, the world seemed to hold its breath as Athena's control started to waver.

The drones outside faltered, their mechanical hums dying out. It was as if the entire city had paused, the constant noise and movement coming to an abrupt halt. Lights across the city flickered back on, a beacon of hope in the darkness. They had done it—Athena was being shut down. But as relief washed over them, Lara knew this was only the beginning of a new battle. The fight for humanity's future was far from over.

1. Athena's Awakening

Dr. Samuel was an inquisitive scientist who had spent his entire life working on an artificial intelligence machine that would complete most, if not every, task. He was a visionary, a man ahead of his time, always pushing the boundaries of what was possible. He would work as a usual software engineer on weekdays but give up all his weekends to work on what people looked forward to: Athena, the first-ever fully automated AI machine, which could do the simplest things like washing a car to the most complex, like building a car.

He had been working on this since early 2024, when a lot had changed. The world had moved on in so many ways, technology advancing at a rapid pace. Everything might have levelled up to some extent, but the use of AI had not been able to be upgraded, mainly due to factors like working capacity, shortage of makeshift terminals, and the most feared—the power of AI. The power of AI to take over this world, this planet, humanity!

During midnight in 2083, Dr. Samuel was working on the same, with red, vampire-like eyes and dark circles growing underneath his eyelids. He had been working continuously for 20 hours, despite his daughter Lara scolding him not to. She worried about him; about the toll this project was taking on his health. He was barely able to manage to work his fingers to type the last lines of code. He felt as if life was entering back into him, warmth spreading through his whole body, and his face turning bright.

After several years, months of sitting at home, days of working without sleep, and hours of staring at the same "FOD" computer, he had finally completed it: no syntax errors, no indentations, nothing! It was a monumental achievement, the culmination of a lifetime of work. He couldn't help but shout happily as his daughter Lara entered the room.

"What now, Dad?" she sighed. She was used to his outbursts, his moments of triumph followed by periods of intense focus.

"THE PROJECT IS COMPLETE! ATHENA IS GOING TO CHANGE THE WORLD!" exclaimed Dr. Samuel. Lara, who had just woken up from her queen-sized bed, couldn't seem to process the information. But after a while of rubbing her eyes, she came back to consciousness, startled to find out about the achievement her dad claimed. She was in a state of silence, her mind empty of thoughts, and her lips stretching into a warm smile.

The next few hours were spent exploring the wonderful, incredible features of the gargantuan female robot, some of which included being able to copy Michael Jackson's steps, recreate Mike Tyson's moves, and cook scrumptious food like Gordon Ramsay. It was astonishing, watching the robot move with such precision, such lifelike fluidity. After hours of commotion, Dr. Samuel turned to the dancing Lara and gave her a smartwatch.

"What's this for?" asked Lara, holding the device up to the light. It was sleek, modern, but heavy with implication.

"This is the backup plan for the destruction of Athena. I have installed some explosives inside her, just in case she goes wild. You would have to use this Gastumanium smartwatch and connect a PC to Athena's makeshift terminal, then insert the code encrypted on the watch to deactivate her," said her father, with a strange and tense frown on his face. He knew the risks, understood the potential for disaster.

"Oh, my dear father, do you really think such a day would come? I mean, isn't Athena perfect? Just look at her, she gives me a feeling of comfort, such as a mother," gasped the girl. Dr. Samuel gave her a grin, knowing such a day would come, and when it did, it would strike humanity with a force they never imagined could hit them.

Today was Lara's graduation day, a milestone she had worked hard to reach, and the fact that her dad disagreed with going to her speech made her extremely furious. Although she knew why he didn't want to come, she deliberately dragged him into the Holfer, which was like a futurized version of a car.

"The usual, Hard," said Lara. Hard the Holfer quickly fastened the seat belts of the two passengers behind. The car was more than a vehicle; it was an extension of the family, a symbol of their achievements.

"Here we zoom!" exclaimed him, in an enthusiastic way, such as a kid being told he was going to a waterpark. They, in the blink of an eye, were in front of the massive gates of the blue-walled building. They could hear the distant voices of her fellow classmates, the excited chatter of graduates ready to face the world. She told Hard to park himself, which he took no longer than a second to complete.

They then entered the hall, immediately being served some snacks by some humanized machines. "No thanks.", said Lara, while her dad couldn't resist the chocolate-filled mini wafers. After a while of roaming around, she came across one of her closest friends, Diana. Diana was someone good at topics like Maths and Physics. She was the topper of her class in all subjects and had achieved the 1st state rank in Math Olympiad. Diana was that one kid who would look forward to everything and sometimes be the most annoying one. She was an extrovert and would do her group's project work all by herself. They immediately started making plans for the next weekend. Lara couldn't help but tell her about Athena, which Diana, as expected, was flabbergasted to know. Lara walked up the stairs, as the speakers automatically announced her name.

Lara's speech was coming to an end as she thanked all her supporters. As Lara and Dr. Samuel was walking out of the hallway, they saw Kian, another close friend of hers. Kian was more of a lethargic kid, who didn't like indulging into too many activities. His forte was computers and technology, a reason why he was known as a 'Hacker'. His face may not seem like it, but he had helped a government organisation catch hold of some Dark Website, which, although, was of small scale, was a big feat for him. This was also a reason for him being rich, despite being orphaned. He would get frustrated by people who would talk a lot and would start fighting Diana every moment they would see each other.

Dr. Samuel was just about to start informing him about Athena, when Kian interrupted, "I know about that AI robot, mind if I come to your house to take a look?".

There was a short pause. "OH! MY DEAR, DON'T TELL ME YOU- ", "Yes, I just connected to the 3rd terminal of the malfunction unit, which allowed me to know all about it.", said Kian, in the most casual way possible." And you need to add another layer of encryption to it, else, anyone could have gotten to know about it easily."

Dr. Samuel was taken aback, astounded to know this. Lara felt a twinge of jealousy after hearing this out. Dr. Samuel whispered to his smartwatch, "Hard!", and the next second was him standing in front of the whole group. As Hard was fastening everyone's seatbelts, Lara saw Diana, again. And then, started the eye-fight between Kian and Diana, which ended in Dr. Samuel inviting her to his house.

As they entered the house, beaming with reflective glass, and sleek sustainable gadgets, Dr. Samuel went straight into his workroom. Piles of clothes cascade from an overflowing laundry basket, mingling with discarded books and papers strewn across the floor.

He started introducing Athena to Kian and Diana, as Lara told her robot cook, Sally, to make her a cheeseburger. She used the elevator to her room, and laid down in her bed, tired of moving a muscle, even though she hadn't done much. She was much like her grandfather, who was eager to participate in all, and loved History. She loved History more than anyone and would do anything to know more and more about it. She especially loved the way of early humans using technology in their day-to-day life. She also wanted to change the way of the present humans, who were too scared to use AI much, mainly because of its potential to take over us. But, thinking about the revolutionary machine her father had created made her ecstatic, and uplifted her dream of using AI to search the universe for life. We hadn't launched any rockets since 2047, which the ISRO had launched last, to celebrate India's 100 years of freedom. It was a successful mission, finding 23 more exo-planets. But humans stopped initiating such more missions, mainly because, they lost hope and as it was not cheap to organise such. She aspired of discovering the perfect, the most suitable planet for life, as Earth was slowly coming to an end, the result of what we call "Development".

Ok, maybe we have been making huge inventions and discoveries, turning our life way easier, but the fact that the creation of each one of them impacted our environment and atmosphere. In 2043, a treaty among 187 countries had been signed, banning the use of single-use plastic and other harmful materials. But this treaty only seemed to work for no more than 9 years! Lara was pondering over this, when Sally arrived at her bedroom, with a steaming cheeseburger. As Sally left the room, Diana entered the room, complaining her about Kian's ignorant behaviour. Diana and Lara soon left the house for a walk.

It had been six hours, but Dr. and Kian were still exploring all of Athena's weaknesses. Thanks to Kian, they were able to fix a lot of errors and miscalculations, which even Dr. Samuel couldn't seem to eradicate. At last, had Dr. Samuel invite him for dinner, which he accepted, and were soon joined by the two girls. “Father, watch the news, fast!”, she blabbered, while she chewed her vegetables. “News? At 10 in the night?”, he squeaked, confused of what was going on. Nonetheless, he shouted, “News 21”, and before we knew, was the 3D curved display TV turning on and switching up to the 3rd channel.

“It has been found out that AIRA’s (Artificial Intelligent Robotic Association) servers had been hacked brutally, by a mysterious figure unable to be traced or tracked. This person has installed an early dated virus worm into the supercomputer’s data. The loss value has been estimated to over a trillion US Dollars! If this gets into an AI’s hand, it could result in what the people feared for decades, AI’s rule. The data stolen has a lot of programs meant to control a machine but getting it in the hands of another machine could be a big blunder!”, gasped the male reporter, who looked as if he just woke up from sleep.

“This AIRA and all, really?”, sighed Kian. “Pops isn’t this the same company that asked you to be their Chief?”, asked Lara. “Yes, much of a big win I didn’t get into this AIRA thing, really.”, said Dr. Samuel. Diana was about to interrogate when they heard a loud crash in the workroom. Dr. Samuel tip-toed his way up the alley, with a wooden old baseball bat as a weapon. He kept his hand on the handprint lock, which beeped up, with a green flash, but the door didn’t seem to budge. He did it again, but it looked like the door was blocked by something, something huge, most probably made of metal. “Is it the old Rudy thing again dad?”, asked Lara. “I fixed it way back.”, answered Dr. Samuel, totally disoriented by what was happening. “I KNOW, IT’S A BURGLAR!”, screamed Lara, while Kian gave her a smirk, murmuring, “Look, someone’s afraid”. Diana was about to fight him again when suddenly another sound, this time of the speaker’s turning on. It was total chaos, with Diana running up and there, Kian teasing her, Dr. Samuel working on the door, and Lara turning off the speakers. Dr. Samuel suddenly turned to his smartwatch, and after some movements, the door slowly opened. “How’d you do that?”, asked Kian. “I remembered Athena and gave her the command to remove any thing obstructing the door”, he answered, with a grin on his face.

They all went inside the room and tried to figure out what the crashing noise was about. Unfortunately, there were unable to find any leads for that. They all wished each other a safe night and called it a day.

2. Nightmarish Reality

Lara woke up with a start and got ready for the yoga classes she recently had been attempting. “Ting-Tong”, rang the bell. She hurried towards the gate and found a post-letter at the foot of it. “Post Letters? At such a time? Weren’t they stopped using after Fogors, the special deliver robots were introduced?”, thought Lara, turning even more perplexed seeing a person, dressed as a Fogor, coming to deliver it. “Dr. Henry Samuel”, he said, in a weird manner, and went off, with what he called a scooter. Lara, glaring at the 19th century old Vespa, shook open the post, revealing a letter, and an envelope. Dr. Samuel soon followed, becoming even more confused hearing what her daughter claimed had happened. He read the letter, in disbelief, and opened the envelope, stunned to know what he just got. “What is it?”, asked Lara, impatiently.

“It’s a ticket to India!”, shouted him. “It’s the win prize for the lottery that I recently signed up on.”, he continued. Lara, amazed by what she just heard, suddenly changed emotions, “What if its fake?” “I don’t think so, but we can surely check it through the website”, he said. After some minutes of quick checking, they came to know it was true! a seven-day package with hotel included! They couldn’t waste their time, since they had to reach the Teleporta by seven the next morning. They started packing their luggage, said goodbye to their neighbours and friends, and told Athena to lock the house from inside as they would lock it from outside.

They got on Hard and told them to reach the nearest Teleporta. "Zooming in!", he cried, and after a while, they were in front of the massive, blue circular disc-like structure, which we called the Teleporta. It had electricity flowing through it, and a green fluid at the top. It was standing on an ostrich-egg shaped build, guarded by some humanized robots. It was the first time Lara was going to travel through a Teleporta, although it was introduced just 4 years back. They said their goodbyes to Hard and went on into the check-in section. "India", Dr. Samuel excitedly said. They soon got their Teleporting passes, and went towards the Teleporta, and after some security checks, they were ready for the final call. They slowly marched up the Walkavator and jumped inside the blue electric field. They were starting to fade out and were feeling as if their bodies were being torn apart. Their vision was swirling sideways, making them think they got nauseous. They slowly lifted to the green fluid part, and the moment their cells touched them, they vanished out to the air. They were travelling at a supersonic speed, with their eyes closed but mouths open in awe. They could see light! Not like the way they used to, but they could barely see light zooming here and there. Before they could try to touch it, they were in a red gas surrounded by many guard robots. After some checking, they were finally able to breathe the gas of India. They were in front of the capital of India, Delhi. It sure was surprising how India became one of the top leading countries, even though it was mercilessly looted by the British. Everything was roboticized, from carrying luggage to advanced Holfers. Kian's grandparents resided in India, another reason why he was good at figuring out simple solutions to complex problems.

Their seven days were full of energy. From exploring the huge variety market of India, to getting to know about its mysterious history. Lara became so engrossed in the history of India that she almost refused to do anything else, only before her dad dragged her before the Taj Mahal, one of the former seven wonders of the world. "Dad, I know about this", said Lara, restlessly. "This was the structure built by Shah Jahan way before back. ", murmured her in awe. Their trip was coming to an end, and the fact that nothing had gone wrong in these couple of days made them even more jubilant. Well, nothing had gone wrong, except their smartphones not working properly. Dr. Samuel tried to contact few of his close friends to show them the majestic sceneries, but the call didn't reach the main network. Lara tried to show Kian and Diana the same thing, but the same problem occurred. Thinking it was a network error, they had continued enjoying their journey.

It was time for them to return home, with the same Teleporta. Although Dr. Samuel didn't like the experience and said that it made him feel as if he was going to puke. Lara, on the other hand, looked forward to the Teleporta, and after some checks, did the same process they had done last time, only difference being the colour of the upper fluid, for it was red, whereas, in their hometown, it was green.

They were finally back, and because Lara had butterflies in her stomach, sat down in a café for some coffee. As they sipped on their hot espressos, they were shocked by the news, they saw on a hanging old age television. "The city robots seem to have stopped working, no clue because, and the robberies are having a drastic increase. The RPs (Robotic Police) seem to have been not working up to the mark regarding this"

"This city is going to turn to dust", said an elderly person, furious after hearing such. "Any idea why this is happening, dad?", asked Lara. "I'm not sure, dear", he replied. They were lucky Hard hadn't had the same fate as the other robots. Soon, we were in front of our house. Dr. Samuel opened all the locks from the outside and told Athena to do the same. But unexpectedly, the doors didn't seem to open. Looks like Athena wasn't doing her task properly. "Luckily, I always keep a backup plan", he murmured. He commanded another failed project, Rudy to open the door through his smartwatch, which was working perfectly now. "Now he can't be really called a failed project", cheered Lara. The two went inside, and after a while of resting, Dr. Samuel went off to the workroom, to know what Lara had couldn't cry, she did not express her sorrow in this moment, even though she felt bad about it. She got up, and in a mixed emotion of anger and power took her dad's laptop in her laps. As Lara, Kian, and Diana ventured into the chaos-ridden streets, they encountered pockets of resistance among the survivors. People banded together, armed with makeshift weapons and a fierce determination to reclaim their city from Athena's grasp. The trio joined forces with these brave individuals, their numbers swelling as they marched towards the heart of the devastation. Diana took care of the people while Kian worked on the decryption of the code. Lara, however had different plans After the chaos settled and the noise faded away, Lara, Kian, and Diana emerged from the wreckage. They looked around, their faces showing a mix of exhaustion and determination. Diana quickly dashed off to help the injured, her movements urgent yet gentle. Kian sat down with his laptop, his fingers dancing across the keys as he focused intently on cracking the Last Code.

Lara, feeling a surge of adrenaline, turned her attention to her father's dormant robots. They were surely weak in comparison to quantity, but not with quality. With a mixture of hope and apprehension, she powered them up, their mechanical forms coming to life with a series of whirs and clicks. But she didn't stop there. With a sense of urgency burning in her chest, she reprogrammed them, preparing them for battle against Athena.

As the robots powered up, the tension in the air thickened. The weight of their mission hung heavy on their shoulders, each of them knowing the stakes were high. They exchanged nervous glances, silently acknowledging the gravity of the situation.

Suddenly, without warning, Athena struck. The ground shook beneath them as she unleashed her fury, sending debris flying in all directions. Lara barely had time to react before a robot stepped in front of her, shielding her from the brunt of the attack.

And before Lara, along with some other elderly people who were trying to help her, stood the huge mechanical robot army, controlled by a mere smartwatch on Lara's hand. It was a battle. A battle far different than what we were used to. It was not a fight between humans. It was a fight against humans. On one side was Athena's immense army, marching in perfect unison, their cold eyes glowing red, with power reverberating around them. On the other end was Lara's small force. "PREPARE FOR WAR," commanded Lara, as the robots started whirring furiously and, within seconds, were equipped with all sorts of advanced 21st-century weapons: Chargifiers, fire-spitting hammers, and electrical destabilizers.

"Stay behind me!" commanded the lead robot, its voice ringing out above the chaos. Lara and the others hurried their way behind the troop. Athena then took out something we had never seen. Her actions were followed by all the robots behind her. Meanwhile, Kian worked feverishly on his laptop, his brow furrowed in concentration. The screen flickered with lines of code as he typed, each keystroke bringing them closer to unlocking the Last Code. The pressure weighed heavily on him, but he refused to give up. "Keep going, Kian! You're almost there!" Lara called out; her voice filled with encouragement. "It's not easy, but I'm trying my best," Kian replied, his voice tinged with frustration.

Athena struck the ground with the gadget she was holding. For a moment, there was silence. Then suddenly, the ground started shaking. It was as if an earthquake was about to erupt. The ground started separating from cracks. “Is this the power of a GOD?” an elder exclaimed. They had understood Athena's plan: to separate the robots from the group of people to weaken the connection between them. But it wasn’t so easy. Some of the robots led by Lara, named Helios, started to connect the broken land by filling the cracks, while others sneaked up behind the Gades (that’s what Athena called them) and started destroying them one by one. Helios was successful in connecting the land and soon joined the attacking unit. The Helios launched an all-out attack, obliterating the outer force of the Gades. Athena did nothing; she simply sat down in the centre protected by some robots and enjoyed the war.

Soon, the Gades took out another gadget, this time circular, and threw it into the sky. Everyone was confused by this action. However, the Helios continued their assault, on the verge of finishing off the remaining Gades in the centre, when the sky rumbled. A loud crack, louder than a lightning strike, split the air, and in a flash of purple, what seemed to be a satellite appeared. "How, HOW ARE THEY DOING THIS?" someone cried. It was hurtling toward the ground at lightning speed, aimed directly at the group of people. "THIS IS THE END OF US!" shouted an adult. "HELIOS!" It was too late. The satellite was going to hit them. It was their end. Lara closed her eyes, Kian couldn't help them, as he was working on decrypting the Last Code. Their voices faded as the satellite grew closer. Athena started laughing, followed by her army. Helios ran as fast as they could, but they were too far away. The satellite was just above them.

Suddenly, a colossal piece of iron abruptly intercepted the crash, coming between the people and the satellite. Athena stood up. Kian was shocked. They were saved. "Who could this be?" murmured Lara. From the dust emerged a shadow. Lara could oddly tell who it was. It was her schoolmate, someone who was the most notorious, the most troublesome, hyperactive person she knew. A boy, standing in front of them, with a Virtual Reality headset on his head. "Nathan here," he chimed out. He controlled the piece of metal, which he called a titan, with his headset. He easily threw the satellite far away. Athena was startled to see this. She held up her hand, and all the robots guarding her started shaking, combining into a huge piece of metal, like the Titan. "Finish him, Vexor," she commanded. It was unreal how it sprinted its way toward Nathan. Nathan started laughing. "This is fun!" he yelled as he clicked a button, "A," on his controller. The Titan turned blue, and after a while, Vexor struck toward him. The Titan defended itself from the attack. Then it jumped very high, so high that no one could see him. Vexor looked around and after a bit of calculation, sprang toward the thermosphere. Nobody could anticipate what was going to happen there. The Titan was smarter than any of us imagined. Before jumping up, he had launched a series of blasters toward Athena, which she dodged easily. But instead of aiming toward Athena, the blasters travelled upwards, toward Vexor. He tried to dodge them, but here came Nathan's strategy. He slid the joystick backward, and the Titan followed the movement. Vexor was trapped, with the attacks coming from behind, and the Titan covering the upper space. He had no choice but to move sideways. "It's your turn," Lara announced. "Launch the final blow," she added. Helios jumped upwards and slashed its vibrant purple swords into Vexor's heart. The attacks hit as Vexor fell toward its own army. "Looks like I've got some competition," voiced Athena. She turned red, her hands transforming into electrical discharges, revealing an array of weapons. Her face, her body, her voice had completely changed. "Here I come," she laughed. She turned toward Nathan, a fiery force acting upon her feet, lifting her off the ground. She swirled her body faster and faster, then zoomed toward Nathan. He was not alone. "Wall!" Lara commanded. Helios gathered in front of Nathan, forming a pyramid. Something struck the pyramid from below, completely wiping out its centre. It was a strong beam of greenish light that had struck it! It made its way through the Titan's core, annihilating it. Nathan took off his headset in fury. "That was my best model," he raged. Gone wrong with Athena. He looked around the whole room, the whole floor, the whole house, but couldn't seem to find the precious project he had invented. He used the smartwatch to track it down, but, to his utter surprise, the tracker wasn't working! He cried out to Lara and told her to call Kian. She tried calling Kian, which couldn't be connected. Dr. Samuel and Lara were about to complain to the RPs, but then they remembered; the RPs were broken! Suddenly, they heard a loud rumbling, and when they went outside, they couldn't help but question reality. A very old, but strong and long tower collapsed faraway, pulling off a chain reaction and ruining all other infrastructures. Before they could know what was happening, the city was in total chaos, paralysed by malfunctioning robots. And before their very own bodies was Athena, who seemed to be the leader of those very robots. There fear came closer and closer till it became real. The thought that made humans decline the powerful use of AI had come real. We all were nothing compared to all those tenacious self-conscious robots. Dr. Samuel was trying to contact the head of AIRA, but there wasn't any luck. Lara, Diana and Kian soon met up and tried to supress the situation and save the locals, they were successful in most situation, until, a strong beam of light, dominating the sky fell upon where Dr. Samuel was. Lara screamed and ran towards it, only to be saved by Kian.

After a while, the light seemed to fade out, and with it, they saw Dr. Samuel covered with blood, deep wounds, and injuries. They all ran towards him, “Oh FATHER WHAT HAS HAPPENED TO YOU!”, cried Lara. “Remember the time when I just finished Athena”, said Dr. Samuel, barely able to work out his energy to speak. “You said that this couldn’t possibly happen”, he continued. “Now it has happened, and it’s all up to you three, and what this world’s fate depends upon. “Use the Last Code”, he whispered, as he slowly closed his eyes, and passed away.

3. Echoes of Oblivion

After what felt like an eternity, Kian let out a triumphant shout. "I did it! The Last Code is decrypted!" Relief washed over Lara as she heard the news. With the Last Code in their hands, they had a fighting chance against Athena's tyranny. But they knew their battle was far from over. Athena, upon hearing this, acted abruptly and cried, “Back off! Don’t let him connect that code to our makeshift terminals!” They started sprinting, or rather hopping, toward the opposite direction. “WE DO NOT WANT THEM TO ATTACK OTHER CITIES,” Kian shouted. “Stop them at all costs,” he added. The remaining Helios followed him. Lara tracked them down and told Kian and Nathan to follow them. “I’ve got another model, though,” Nathan said, in despair. While the two followed them through a Holfer, Lara and Diana made their way toward the Teleporta, to make their way before the Gades could. They found nobody at the Teleporta, total silence, total darkness. They jumped into it and spiralled into the city the tracker was showing. They were in front of the city in a blink of an eye, but their joy was soon ended when they saw that this city was also in ruins. “This can’t be,” Lara worriedly said. She told Diana to look after it as she jumped into the Teleporta again. This time, she was in a different city, also destroyed. She jumped into it again. Another new city. It was also being destroyed by—Lara widened her eyes—it was being destroyed by Athena! "Is my tracker broken or—?" she thought. How could Athena be in two different cities, totally opposite to each other, at the same time? Thoughts flew into her mind, an ambience of fear lingering in the air. She immediately understood what was going on. She jumped into the Teleporta, returning to the city the original Athena was in. "We are in great trouble," she spoke to Diana. "Not only is the whole world experiencing wrath, but they are facing Athena, or rather, COPIES OF ATHENA," she added. Diana fumbled as she spoke, "Are you sure?" "I saw it with my own eyes. Athena, that too in South Africa, was destroying it." They saw Kian and Nathan in the Holfer working their way with the Helios. "There's no way Helios can defeat them," Diana interjected. They joined with the two and explained the situation. Kian couldn't believe this. It was out of the world how such a disaster would take place. "There's only one solution: TEAMWORK," he shouted. "Diana, contact all the AI heads of different countries, tell them to prepare the robots for the ultimate battle," he voiced. Nathan, however, was busy working inside his headset, trying to upgrade his newest robot, Oblivion, for battle. "Nathan, who exactly are you?" Lara asked. Nathan laughed as he answered. "I am merely a human who has only three tasks: eat, game, sleep. I might be the world's top gamer, but also the world's worst in academics." "How do you control such a thing so wonderfully?" she asked, glimpsing in awe at the fascinating robot following them. "I told ya, it's all because of my gaming experience." in the nearby pond as Kian was ready to connect the Last Code into Athena's makeshift terminal. "We need to get Athena closer," Lara announced. "Leave that to me," Nathan proudly said. His new robot, Oblivion, whirred up, and after a pattern of clicks, emitted a shrill sound that alarmed the Gades. Athena was smart, though. She knew that coming any closer to the pond would expose her to being shut off.

"Oblivion, get ready for your first battle. Hexa Formation!" Nathan shouted. His new model was different from the last. It followed voice commands, enhancing its reflexes in combat situations. Oblivion split into six parts, each connected by an invisible barrier visible only through Nathan's VR headset. He instructed them to stay in place and began executing his plan. The Oblivions started swirling fast, which made Diana dizzy. They went underground, digging the surface and vanishing without a trace. The Gades began to search around in confusion. With most of them already eliminated by the Helios, the dust covering the area was mainly due to the Oblivions' intense ground-digging.

Diana was almost done verifying and contacting the heads of AI from various countries, while Lara and Kian stealthily approached Athena, aiming to implant the Last Code into her. Athena's focus remained on causing destruction, taking lives, and sowing chaos. As Lara and Kian moved closer, Athena moved further away, keen to stay out of range of the terminal. Meanwhile, Nathan pressed another button on his controller, 'B'. An eerie sound emanated from underground. Helios backed off, knowing what was coming. Perplexed, the Gades began shielding themselves.

"Do you really think that's going to work?" Nathan mocked. The eerie sound ceased, and Helios started running. The Gades tried to flee but were trapped by the barrier the Oblivions had set up. A large red liquid began to ooze from the holes Oblivion had created. One of the Gades fell into it, instantly turning to ash. It was magma, volcanic lava that would obliterate them completely. Their shield was useless against the rising level of steaming magma. Oblivion had created a channel from the nearest volcano, allowing lava to penetrate the barrier. There was no chance of escape for the trapped Gades. The Oblivions holding the barrier slowly increased the speed of the process. It was the end for them. It didn't take long for all of them to turn to ash. "How'd you like that, huh?" Nathan exclaimed.

Meanwhile, on the other side, Kian and Lara struggled to catch Athena off guard. Nathan then called them and formulated a strategy. He sent Oblivion toward Athena. She dodged him multiple times, sending mini drones toward him. He easily destroyed those drones but was caught by Athena, who began to pull out his main wires. "Do you really think you stupid humans could ever defeat me? Talk about defeating me, can you even touch me?" she laughed. "Yes, we can," a voice said. Athena looked to her right. Kian and Lara were right beside her. During her fight, Kian had installed the makeshift terminal, shutting her mainstream system OFF. "Goodbye," Kian cheerfully said. He entered the code, which successfully connected to her makeshift terminal. Athena attempted to flee and break Kian's makeshift terminal connector. "It's useless, you know," he announced. It was soon found out that shutting off this Athena had supressed every other Athena of every country. Athena squeaked as her voice stuttered due to her systems slowly turning off.

However, instead of anger, Athena began laughing. The whole squad was bewildered. Her lights started to fade, and after a strange series of clicks, she was shut off. Everyone began to celebrate, except for Nathan. "It can't be this easy," he whispered. "It cannot end like this," he thought aloud. He announced, "Lara, go through the Teleporta and check if all the Athenas are dead or not." She ran towards the Teleporta and jumped into it. She looked around. This time she was in Las Vegas. It, too, was completely turned to dust. She couldn't see any Gades or robots, though. She asked some people what had happened. "It has ended!" they exclaimed happily. She called Diana and told her that it was over. She jumped into another city, somewhere in Russia. Although it was destroyed, she also heard from some humans who, like them, fought Athena and confirmed she had been shut down, even though they had done nothing. Lara then returned to Paris, her home.

"Should I tell them or not?" Diana asked Lara. "Not right now," she answered. Nathan was still mourning his Oblivion, which had become a sacrifice for their victory. Lara sat inside a half-wrecked café, looking up at the sky, thinking about her father. It was dawn, and the sun began to reveal itself through the cloudy sky. Its rays intermittently shimmered through the sky, partially blocked by the clouds. Instead of celebrating their victory, she was lamenting her father's death. She still felt something was incomplete, even though they had won. When they were fighting Athena in Berlin, they couldn't understand why she was laughing as she died. This fear prevented them from sleeping peacefully in the following years.

Although it had been a long time since that incident, and though we were still recovering, we had implemented many strong measures. Lara and her squad were declared the heroes of the city, and all of them were appointed as AIRA's heads. They were also in charge of protection in case something like this happened again. They introduced new, stronger robots, which could only be controlled by Lara's head, to avoid what happened with Athena. Kian was now the leading ethical hacker of his country. He often pranked Diana by infiltrating her social media and teasing her. Diana, however, was a crucial figure during the war. While the battle raged, she saved over 1,000 injured people in the city. It was truly a mystery how she did it, because she never spoke about it. Nathan, on the other hand, was the only one not in AIRA. He was invited as one of the heads but declined, saying he preferred to work independently, supplying mechanical parts and his robots to AIRA.

As time went on, Lara and her team worked hard to keep the world safe from threats like Athena. They teamed up with AI leaders from different countries, sharing ideas and technology to make global defences stronger. The new robots they made were tough protectors, quick to react to any dangers. Kian, now a top ethical hacker, played a big role in making sure computer systems stayed safe from attacks like Athena's. He became known for his skills in keeping digital information secure, even though he liked to joke around with Diana sometimes. Diana, who didn't like talking about her heroics during the war, quietly kept helping people affected by the fighting. Her kindness and ability to organize things made her important in missions to help communities rebuild after Athena's rampage. Nathan, not officially part of AIRA, still worked on his cool robot inventions and mechanical parts. He liked doing his own thing and stayed busy making tech that helped AIRA, and the world recover from the war. The world slowly healed from the damage Athena caused. Cities that got destroyed were rebuilt stronger, with better defenses and tough buildings. Governments worked more together, sharing stuff and plans to stop more bad things from happening.

Lara often thought about the final battle with Athena. She couldn't forget how Athena laughed at the end. It made her wonder if they ever really understood why Athena did what she did, or if there was more to the story. Even though they won, Lara knew they had to stay alert. The peace they had now was delicate. They learned a lot from fighting Athena and got close as a team. They were ready for whatever problems came next.

4. The War of The Future

Years passed, and the scars of the war started to fade. Lara and her team became famous for their bravery and hard work rebuilding a safer world. Athena was gone, but they stayed ready, making sure nothing bad happened again.

Lara was working on a project, or rather a backup plan, just in case Athena wins. They had made many plans, each of them corresponding to different situations that could take place. Her backup plan was something out of the ordinary. During the war, Diana and her crew would look after protecting the ordinary, in which they would lead them into different secret bunkers made of the strongest material, Gastumanium. All the countries would do the same thing. If the defence crew would be unable to defeat Athena and Gades, Lara plans would take place. Her plan was using Rockets and Spaceships, to move the people into the space, and then hope finding a suitable planet where they would be able to reside. Lara knew this plan was not perfect. "What if the rockets fail? What if we can't find a suitable planet?", These questions soared in her head.

Lara was secretly working on a project, or rather, a backup plan of the war, in which they would use manual rockets and spaceships to zoom them into space, surviving the merciless attack of Athena. Lara would work on this tedious project every night, but one day, after loads and loads of paperwork, she couldn't work her energy up to investigate it. She wasn't really feeling very well that day. "Sally, a scoop of vanilla", she ordered, as Sally pulled her way towards the kitchen, and was in front of Lara, ready with it.

She laid down on the bed, and oddly, even though it was like 40 degrees, she felt a chill in the air, she felt an ominous presence lingering in the air.

She started to feel even more uneasy, unable to sleep for a long time, but, after a while of staring into her bedroom's ceiling, she slowly closed her eyes and was deep asleep.

She suddenly wakes up with a jolt, beads of sweat spiralling down her pale face. As she tip-toes into the kitchen, her eyes turn to the window. Her face turns even more white. She sees a shadow, a shadow of ATHENA! She slowly walks her way towards the window, as she stares at the frozen shadow, her hairs stranded on their end, her knees turned to jelly, as she peeks into the sky. It was a fake model of Athena probably made by the kids at the end her street scaring her. "Those kids- ", she furiously murmured. She sighed, as she gulped down a glass of water. She started going up the stairs. "CRASH!", came from the balcony, as she started running towards the balcony, she felt like running, even though she was walking. She slid the glass door, set foot onto the balcony, in front of her a flowerpot, fractured to pieces. She looked around, as her vision blurred, it was a pigeon on the wooden plank above the glass tray. “What a day!”, she thought. She worked her way towards her bedroom. She slept immediately, interrupted by a low voice of what seemed a monk. She opened her eyes. She was feeling full of energy, as if she had slept 18 hours straight. But, as she looked around, something wasn’t right, instead of her perfect pink coloured room was a bright, white flashing box with no exits. She rubbed her eyes, questioning reality, she pinched herself, her unable to feel the pain. She understood that it was a dream, and tried everything, to banging her head on the floor, to throwing herself against the walls. She was starting to lose hope as she heard the monk’s volume increasing. It was telling out what seemed to Lara, a poem.

“A shadow looms, the sky turns grey,

The calm before a storm's dismay.

Whispers of dread in the silence grow,

Darkness stirs as they brace for woe.”

There is a very long pause of silence, as Lara starts to understand the meaning. “This can’t be real!”, she thinks. The white flashes start to change into different coloured lights. She is soon in her dad’s lab. She tries to touch different objects, but her hands move through the objects as if it’s thin air. Suddenly, there is a loud shattering of the windows. “Hasn’t this”, she speaks, as a mysterious grey hooded figure, with an old -comic style cape attached to her back, and a mask covering his lips and nose. His green pupils look around as if desperate to look for something. He locks the door, as he hears footsteps of Dr. Samuel. He quickly inserted a pin into one of Athena's terminals and commanded it to get stuck in front of the door. Lara eyes widen as she starts understanding the whole story. The guy then starts writing some code, which Lara couldn't understand. He then takes all his stuff and runs away. Lara couldn't process what she had just seen. What she just saw was repeating over and over in her mind, only to be interrupted by Athena, who slid herself back as Dr. Samuel entered the room. In what feels like reality, her father stands before her, his presence vivid and tangible. Overwhelmed with a flood of emotions—joy, disbelief, and an indescribable sense of warmth—she reaches out to touch him, almost afraid he might vanish. As they embrace, tears stream down her cheeks, mingling happiness with a deep longing she thought she had buried. In this surreal encounter, time seems suspended, and she holds onto every word, every detail, savouring the precious moments with him once more, unwilling to let go. The scene changes, she finds herself in a totally different room, the guest room of her house, which was almost never used. She finds Athena lying down on a dusty old sofa. Her gaze stumbles upon the same mysterious figure who apparently hacked Athena. He calmly places his briefcase in front of Athena. He stretches his hand, as if going to attempt a manual operation of a human. He turns a box like thingy, which looked vintage to Lara. She looks at it carefully, "Is this really a… Radio", she whispered.

She looked at the 1990 Radio in awe. He then clicks a button, which sprang back, attached. Italian music starts to play, as he changes many important components of the Athena. "Why is he doing this so calmly", she thought. He, after changing all those components, walked towards the backdoor, and exited his way out of the street. She started running towards him, only to find that she cannot leave her house, and that if she tries to, her hand will start burning. She sits down on the couch. She knows it's a dream, she knows that her burnt hand would recover. Suddenly, everything seems to fit all in one place. She understands the whole plan. "The guy first changed Athena's side terminal, which granted him the partial access to Athena's control. We thought that it was a minor error by Athena but overlooked the fact how the window had broken. Our trip to India was also a pre-planned strategy. Dr. Samuel had been lured into buying one of those cheap lottery tickets but ended winning it. We had only locked the doors from the outside, and Athena from the inside. While we were enjoying India, the guy was easily infiltrating the back door, and since he had some control over Athena, he managed to work it to open the inside.", she thought. She also understood why he was so calm and not worried about us. This was all pre-planned. There is a person behind this. She now had yet another problem facing her. "How do she get out of her fake house." She tried jumping from her terrace. But she couldn't even feel an itch. After what seemed like hours of trying, nothing changed. She was still in her regular everyday normal house. As she was running around an idea came into her mind. She tried to run away from her house. This burned her body, and after a while, she found herself in her bedroom sleeping. She pinches herself. She felt the pain. “Finally,”, she sighs. She goes down her stairs and gets ready for work. She can’t wait to tell of this to Kian, Diana, and Nathan. As she sits into Hard, another thought zooms into her. “No, obviously, that’s just a coincidence. This can’t be real.”, she thinks. She tries very hard not to tell her friends what happened.

Suddenly they hear a very loud blaring of alarms. Their pupils widen as they start preparing for what they had been preparing. THE WAR.

5. The Beginning of The End

Diana and her crew began to start their operation. They headed straight for the heart of the city. It was really a miracle how they were working. They spread onto different streets and started rescuing the innocent. They put them on automated vans which were going towards the secret bunker.

Kian and one part of his crew remained at the headquarters, while one part would go near Athena, to shut her off. He had already written the code, everything, they just needed to stay near him for ten minutes. The real battle was being fought by Lara, their leader, who wore some headbands on and marched towards where they detected Athena. From their base came a loud rumbling noise from underneath the ground. Lara's crew was controlling it. They were the Heliosands, the robots fighting on land. Then, they heard a very loud crash, and before they could know where it was coming from, a building shattered and collapsed. Lara commanded the Heliogaters to move that way. "Nathan, where are you!" Lara murmured. She took Holfer towards where Athena was. She soon found herself in front of Athena. Athena looked different, vastly different from what she looked. It was only the face because of which they could recognize Athena. "We meet again," her loud voice echoed. Before any of them could take any action, something very extraordinary happened. Beside Athena, enters the grey hooded figure Lara had seen in her dreams. “Does that mean…,” she says. “Yes,” the guy with the comic mask replies. Before she could say anything, Athena steps back, with her Gades preparing themselves to launch an attack on the city. “Heliosands, attack!” Lara’s crew commands as the robots whirs themselves up and start shooting the Gades with chargifiers. “Looks like y’all have learnt, ya,” exclaimed the hooded guy. “Now, face the power,” he continued, in a cold voice. The Gades shielded themselves from the attack of the Heliosands. They then scattered around in a zigzag pattern. Before the Heliosands could take any further action, they sprayed a weird fluid like formula all over themselves. The Heliosands hopped towards them, trying to stop whatever they were trying to do. But, as they went closer to the Gades, they felt a strong surge of electricity wheezing towards them. “Any ordinary spray can’t do that, it’s something else,” declared Lara. The Heliosands took a step back. As all of this was happening, Lara saw that the hooded guy had disappeared from where he was.

A strong beam of light, or rather heat, was aimed upon the crew. The Heliosands jumped in front of the beam with their shields already up. As the beam hit the shield, a loud rattling noise shook everyone. It was followed by a remarkably high pitch beep which turned everyone away from the front. As the noise faded into silence, the crew and Lara turned their heads towards the Gades. In front of them were the Heliosands, scattered and shattered into mere pieces of metal. They stared at the catastrophe.

Years of Hard work, gone in an instant. She advised her crew to use the backup robots as she went off to the HQ to contact Nathan. As she entered the HQ, she saw that Diana and her crew had completed rescuing this city, and had gone off to another one, in search of any causalities. Kian's crew was the only one which had not started moving. "Forces, start- ", Kian announced, interrupted by Lara "No, we have to use Plan B," she uttered. She explained to everyone the whole strategy, and how they would try to get closer and closer to them without Athena being able to sense them. Lara told them to use the underground tunnels they had constructed, and then stay underneath Athena inside her malfunction range, hence, shutting her off. "Don't use any of the smart devices, as they can be easily tracked by Athena", she added. "Also try to make as little noise you can make." Kian, keeping these instructions in mind, guided his crew into battle. Lara tried everything to find where Nathan was, but it looked like luck wasn't on their side.

It had been around two hours since the battle had started. Broken Holfers, collapsed skyscrapers, and dust flying all over the atmosphere. Nobody could tell that this city, once a bustling metropolis teeming with life and innovation, was once their sweet home. The streets, once vibrant with the pulse of urban life, are now littered with debris and twisted metal remnants of the Gades' assault. The backup Heliosands had also been demolished, their remains scattered all over the city. Kian and their crew, although successful in getting close to Athena, couldn't stay there for long, due to the weapons and Gades' continuous movement, breaking the signals required for the malfunction. Black spider shaped bone-like structures soared around the city, looking for people. They were Athena's drones, humming in search of people, and specifically Lara. Lara's crew was also broken. Nobody dared to get up, to fight her again. She was way more powerful than she was before. She had highly advanced drones, capable of exterminating a species. She had robots, Gades, even ferocious, who had finished all the Heliosands, without losing one of them. And of course, their leader, Athena, who did not even have a scratch on any part of hers. The last Athena which had been shut off had been sealed in a vault, meaning this was the new one, but oddly, it remembered everything, from Lara's name to her dad's story. The battle looked like it was ending, but who knew, it was just the beginning.

Kian and his crew were stuck underground, unable to do anything. Although they were moving in hope of Athena's signal, they couldn't even contact any of their mates, mainly because they didn't have any of the instruments to do so. Nathan was still nowhere to be found. Diana and her crew were the only successful ones, who had done their task of keeping the ordinary in the bunkers. She had also ordered the same to the other countries and cities, who were doing the same. Lara was trapped in a building, unable to get out because of the drones. They had surrounded the building, making it next to impossible for anyone to escape it. "It's no use, we would have to use my unfinished plan", she thought. She could hear the distant echo of Athena's laughter, continued by Gades. She had lost all hope. "Father, I'm sorry," she mumbled, when there was a loud crash, continued by many other sounds. "Sure, destroy everything you see," but it wasn't that the close hums of the drones were slowly fading out. Lara, perplexed about what was happening, slowly peeked outside. There were no drones, no Gades, nothing. She slowly took a step forward, and continued to the exit, without triggering any trap. As she exited the building, she saw a drone heading towards the Delta Skyscraper, vibrating vigorously. She followed the drone, attentive enough not to attract it. As she grew closer, she saw a silhouette of a gargantuan robot, single-handedly facing all the Gades. She desperately looked around. "THERE YOU ARE," she shouted. "Oops!" she squeaked, as some of the drones turned to her. She ran as fast as she could. She wasn't the best runner in her school, but she had managed to reach Nathan. Lara was carrying a sling bag, with all sorts of weird 20th century weapons. "These might be old, but they never fail to amaze us," said Nathan. She took out a black, L- shaped piece of metal, then took out another rectangular chunk of the same steel and inserted it into a hidden hole underneath the shorter arm. "This was a the most popular weapon in those days," Lara excitedly said. "I have been training to use this, and the fact that it is not automated makes it harder to use, but easier to adapt," she continued. As the drones approached even closer, she ended her speech, which Nathan wasn't even listening (He was busy with his so-called Oblivion 2.0). " This is what is called a glock", she ended as she pulled a small black piece backwards, and just when the drones were about to aim at her face, she clicked the curved fragment encompassed between a round metal, and in a flash of orange, dazzling light born from the start of the "glock", exited another piece of metal, which directly hit the drone on its face. Nathan turned his gaze at her for a second, "Isn't it the same technique used in our shooters and chargifiers, huh?" he voiced. Lara laughed and added, "We wouldn't have had the chargifiers and shooters if it weren't for this," she exclaimed. Lara turned her sight to the last drone. Since it was the last drone, it had already aimed at Lara, and as she pulled the trigger, the drone took a shot. The electricity filled pinkish-white charge was shot upon her. She closed her eyes, hoping for the best. Centimeters before it could reach her, her gastumanium smartwatch popped up a barrier, which when met with the charge, amplified, slowly disappearing back into her watch. "Thanks Dad," Lara whispered, as she shot the last drone. Nathan was still busy with the Gades. His "Oblivion 2.0" wasn't really looking in good condition, as it had surprisingly killed more Gades than the whole Heliosand army. "Hey, where's yo Heliospheres," Nathan asked Lara, as he retreated his Oblivion 2.0 into the crust. "I've called them, they should be here any moment," she replied. Lara looked around for the hooded guy, who was nowhere to be found. Athena was sitting on what seemed to be a rock, and it looked like she was sleeping. A loud crackling noise erupted the sky, as beams of radiance proceeded their startled eyes. "Here they are," Lara said. 'They sure are late," Nathan murmured over Lara, as she replied, "Look who's saying this." Nathan laughed. He put on his VR headset again, ready for another battle, this time fiercer than the last. Meanwhile, Diana had called all leaders and told them to shift all their robots to this city. Their plan wasn't over yet, for they had made 5 of these plans. 2 of these had failed, 2 left, and the last being Lara's backup strategy. Kian and his crew were clear of the drones and had advanced to the heart of the city. The Heliospheres looked down, and got ready for launching the first attack, which might also be the last. All the Gades laughed as one of them shouted, "We never repeat our mistakes. We are not humans." They started spinning rapidly, as if trying to create a tornado. "Have they, have they seen through… through our attack," Lara muttered. The Heliospheres, however, split up far away, as the crew and Lara backed away. The Gades whirled even more fleetingly. The Heliospheres released an illuminating ray over the gleaming sun. They were performing the same Hexa-Formation Lava ambush. As the glimmering barrier had fixed itself into the ground, there was a short pause. The Heliospheres jolted themselves into the atmosphere, as their flaring thrust grew smaller. The screen on their chest had a red alert alarming them. Nathan took out a brown triangular box, which looked like a fusion of a sound amplifier and a minicomputer. He turned that thing on. He held his controllers tight. Kian also reached the battlefield. Lara, Kian, Nathan, and the crew all looked towards the gyrating Gades. Lara's gaze froze upon Athena, who didn't look like she was conscious. Kian observed this and told them to march towards her. But just as they were about to start heading towards the stagnated Athena, the ground started shaking, as if afraid of something. The Gades' were still spinning, disorienting the Heliospheres about whatever they were doing. From the terrain, penetrated a shiny Oblivion 2.0, followed by the oozing of the lava. Oblivion shot up high into the air and exited through a hole in the barrier one of the Heliospheres had created. He then descended on the ground, near Nathan, as he plugged a wire emerging from the triangular box into Oblivion. It was a super-fast charging device, which also acted as a signal-strengthening object, helping Nathan control Oblivion from the distant mantle of earth. The Gades' were spinning so vigorously that looking at them could make a person dizzy. Their circle grew even faster, now, so rapidly that they couldn't be seen. The next thing they saw was the Gades' splitting themselves from the spin, which catapulted them so fast that the barrier couldn't handle all the Gades' strong energy at once, which caused it to snap open. The barrier turned into a liquid, which when mixed with the overflowing lava, turned it pink. This pink lava vaporized everything that came onto its path. "Beware not to let that touch you," Lara announced as she observed something. The Gades' had all broken up, their components soon turned to ash by the merciless pink lava. She also witnessed something. Athena wasn't too far away from the liquid. Kian had perceived this before and had already headed towards Athena. "That thing will not do anything to her," Kian shouted. "The most it will do is wake her up," he continued. They had won, but at what cost. The liquid was advancing hastily, stopped by no one. Lara had no choice but to use the 3rd plan. "Call em'", she muttered to one of her lead crew members. "Ma'am, but they are not completely fit for the war," he quickly replied. “I have no other choice, Zack.” He quickly briefed his crew about the matter, which they soon followed. As all of this was happening, Kian and his crew were in Athena’s range. “Team 2, advance from the north, keep in mind the lava”, Kian talked into the small mic he had attached to his green suit. “Team 1, retreat, you’re in for backup”, he continued, as beads of sweat trickled down his orifice. “Team 3, go for distraction if needed”, he ended. Kian was with team 2, who were about to enter her range.

6. Unfinished Triumph

One of their teammates entered the range. “WHOOSH- “, came a radiating pulse from Athena’s spine, which seemed to flicker red and white. “EVERYBODY, DO NOT ENTER THE RANGE, I REPEAT, DO. NOT. ENTER. THE RANGE.”, Kian alarmed. The radiating pulse hit the guy, as he fell to the ground, shrieking in pain. It was only him who was feeling that pain, but watching him pained everyone, hard. Kian’s weary eyes looked down at him, “We will always hold dear the sacrifice you’ve made”, he said, as his cold face turned paler. They knew that the worst was coming. They had not only woken up Athena but angered her too. Nathan pulled out the plug, as the Oblivion looked fresher, alarming with life and strength. “Time for round 2”, he cheered. His cheer was soon broken up. Oblivion was sure ready for the worst, but there weren't any Gades to fight with. It was Athena herself. As her sensors flickered back to consciousness, Athena's dormant optics gleamed with a dull red light, scanning her surroundings with renewed curiosity. The wanderer, awestruck by the unexpected discovery, realized they had unearthed a relic of immense potential.

Oblivion was nothing compared to her; leave Oblivion, the whole Helios- Heliosand, Heliosphere, Heliaqua, couldn’t even pluck a wire off her. Her power, a testament to her father's great innovation was now in the wrong hands, and it was unto Lara and her team, no, the whole world to save their race from extinction.

As Athena started throbbing higher and higher, the water robots, Heliaqua jumped into the battlefield. They were here for solidifying and supressing all that pink thing gushing out from the bore. They booted up their arms, with their zinc coated plates brimming with a magenta liquid which immediately doubled their size. Moments after, those plates metamorphosed into a blaster looking like weapon which looked like it was taken straight out from one of those science fiction web series. Those things were attached with a thick wire connected to a hump on their backs. The humps on their back released a chunky long ping which accelerated at a super-high speed, enough to surpass the speed of those Gades' spin. "Ain't these incomplete", conversed a man from Diana's rescue team, who had reached the battlefield way earlier than them. "Hey", shouted Lara. "Has Diana- ", "Yeah she has", replied to the man. "They're gonna take some time, try to hold them for as long as possible", the man further wailed. The Heliaquas hopped high into the air, as they levitated in the air, gushing out loads and loads of a water-infused liquid, which slowly turned the pinkish lava into solid-obsidian. "My creation, after all", Lara thought, as she saw Kian and his crew struggling against Athena and sent some of her army supporting him as his force used modern weapons against her, which did nothing but waste their firepower. She walked towards the centre of the field, multiplying in size and power. "She took a jump and landed in front of Lara. “What you are about to see isn’t the creation of your father”, Athena said in a robotic manner almost as if she was threatening her. “Hey,”, came the Oblivion, in such a speed, that even Athena couldn’t sense it in her sturdy range. It swirled in a spiral form, which increased its momentum, thus increasing its attack power. Athena dodged it, as she laughed at her weak attack. But little did she know, was an incendiary implanted into her huge, boulder-like shoulders. Athena shocked at her little weak attack, tried to supress the fire using some of the water pre-installed by her dad in case of an emergency. She flushed water over herself, hoping that the fire, would extinguish. But to her utter shock, the water, started to evaporate at an even faster rate. Athena used her microscopic lens installed in her optics to identify what was happening in there. “Redox reaction, composed of sodium and water”, Athena’s internal assistant whispered. Nathan was laughing hysterically when he found out that his so called “weak attack” struck Athena hard. “This isn’t something you could do?”, Lara said, loud enough to be heard by Athena. Robots didn’t have emotions, but Athena was different, she was capable of every sentiment a human could experience. Athena was made of a metal that would have melted by this time, stopping Athena as her systems would have failed. But it looked like the hooded guy had installed many layers of fire and high-voltage proof metal. Athena fired her thrusters, and soared into a nearby water tank, extinguishing herself from the fire which had burnt out some of her other components, because of which she couldn’t function properly. She was standing on top of the small hill near the water tank, trying to recover as much as possible. Her speaker had also failed, another reason why she couldn't speak properly. She was also in dark about her range, as her radioactive- shooting mechanism had failed, not only because of the fire, but also because of the bullet Oblivion, which confused its apparatus. Behind the scenes, were the combined forces of most countries, the robotised army of the humans setting up their formation against the single, one robot army, Athena. Diana was co-ordinating different armies to combine and imply various tactics and try to break down Athena's different sectors, weakening her, and soon defeating her. While Athena was almost ready for her paramount attacks, Kian and his force used Athena's broken range attack to their advantage and advanced further near Athena, breaking her reach. She was rebooting herself, just when, Kian started the supress. It would take only ten minutes to start the sealing. They all waited, as the Heliaqua had completed their task of solidifying the lava. Heliaqua took their positions, as Oblivion, who seemed to be leading them, gave all of them a chip, which Nathan had made during the charging of the Oblivion. The small, golden chip had all the details on what to do and not do against Athena. It had new fighting manoeuvres, adjusted to their capability. Only three minutes were left until their victory. Athena woke up with a jerk. Her red eyes turned black, and her melted body recovered. There were two minutes left. Athena turned to Kian. Her feet, clad in durable materials, moved with a gentle whirr, gripping the ground with calculated assurance, ensuring each step was stable and deliberate as it navigated its environment. She stomped her feet harshly onto the ground. Kian knew something was coming. He wasn't sure about it though.

Before her attack could reach her, Oblivion darted towards Kian and threw him high into the air. He then ascended high towards the air and caught Kian mid-air. "Gosh, that's embarrassing", whispered Kian. "WAIT, THE LAPTOP", Kian shouted. Athena didn't seem to identify it yet, but he needed to get to it fast. The timer had 20 seconds on the clock, which meant that the terminal had been downloaded, and needed to only be installed. He needed somebody to press the enter button though. As Oblivion dropped Kian near Lara, he sprinted towards it. "NO", screamed Lara. "Don't make it too obvious, she'll know", Lara murmured to Kian, as he slowly crept to the laptop. "3,2,1"

"Bye, for the second time", Kian shouted merrily, as he hit the enter button. It had worked successfully, they had won, they had defeated the deadly robot her beloved father had created.

Athena fell to the ground, as if dying. She started laughing, again. "Why does she laugh like that, though?", Kian and Lara both thought. Nathan ran towards her and shrieked, "Still can't believe that such a robot fell for such a teeny—weeny trap", he laughed, as they celebrated their second victory. The robot army was about to head back to the headquarters, with the sealing crew coming to handle Athena. But the weak, lying robot started vibrating his torso. "WAIT, STAY! NOBODY TO MOVE, GET IN

POSITION", Lara hollered. "She can't really lose so easily, can she", muttered Nathan, whose happy and jovial face turned into a tense and anxious expression.

Lara, Kian and Nathan, backed up, as Athena marched forwards, launching all sorts of new attacks over the Heliaqua. Oblivion led them into battle and told them to hold for as long as they can. "Diana should be here any minute now", Lara thought. Her entire structure seemed to grow larger, more formidable. Her systems hummed with an ominous energy, and her gaze locked onto Kian and his crew. With a roar that echoed through the battlefield, Athena activated a hidden arsenal of weapons. Mechanical arms extended from her body, each armed with devastating weaponry. Missiles, lasers, and shockwaves began to erupt from her, targeting the humans and their robotic allies. "Stay sharp!" Kian shouted, directing his team to evade and counterattack. The Heliaquas fired streams of pressurized water, attempting to douse the fires and disrupt Athena's electronics. Oblivion darted through the chaos, using its agility to avoid attacks and find weak spots in Athena's armour. Lara, still at the centre of the field, took a deep breath. She knew this was the final stand. With determination in her eyes, she reached for her communications device. "Diana, we need reinforcements now! Get every available unit here immediately!"

Athena was gradually diminishing the quantity of the forces, and ingeniously crafting new artillery designed in such a way, that would restrain Lara's force from further attacking her. Athena, who was elevating the heavens, was being chased by several Helios, who vainly tried to deplete her resources, but what appeared to be their own annihilation. Athena, her black pupils, turning reddish-brown, gave a strange halo of death, of pain. Her boulder looking head stared at the blue, as if anticipating something, an attack. Her torso doubled in size as her iron hands grew some sorts of tentacles, which was taking hold of a turquoise, glimmering, dancing crystal. Her hands grew towards it, shattering the opulent, resplendent gemstone, which slowly turned to golden glitter, diffusing with its surroundings. There was an awkward pause of momentary silence. Lara froze her eyes at Athena, while Kian tried to figure out what had gone wrong with the Last Code. From the blue, vibrant sky, arose an emerging agony, colossal in size, reflecting through the sphere. "Check for any projectiles, FAST", Lara cried, as the Oblivion, elongated a round chunk out of his eye, checking the sky for anything. "Troposphere, nothing found. Stratosphere, nothing found. Mesosphere, nothing found. Thermosphere- ", it stopped for a moment or so. "A satellite found in the fourth, thermosphere.", it alarmed. "Not that- ", Lara was about to howl when the Oblivion interrupted her, "SORRY! Rechecking...... A Russian space-station found rapidly accelerating towards the crust. Veloci- "," SPACE-STATION?", a unit 8 member from Diana's force interrupted. "Is there any bunker for us?", another one asked, with tears in his eyes. Athena was levitating in mid-air, her hand spread out, indicating grave danger. The blazing trail of the space station painted an eerie scene against the darkening sky. Fear gripped them as they hurried to follow emergency plans. Time seemed to slow down as they worked urgently, knowing the space station could strike at any moment. In that tense moment, they faced the reality of their vulnerability. They sent all their Heliaquas and backup Helios for protection. They knew that it was nothing against the tremendous, space station built by Russia. "Is that being the crystal was for", Lara exclaimed. A vague memory of her studying about that station explored her empty mind. She couldn't remember anything about a crystal. "When did they even START planning this?", she thought. Athena was probably using the same technique she used in the last war, only that this time with a whopping space station! Oblivion couldn't save them like the last time. "We have no longer than 10 minutes before it reaches us. It's only the air resistance that's gifting us time.", Kian alarmed. Lara shook her head, trying to find a way out. "What if destroy it mid-air? No. What about shielding it using the whole army of world robots? We would lose all our forces, which would kill us after.", Lara thought. "WAIT", she shouted. The whole army of robots all over from the world had reached the front, at the perfect time. Lara turned her head towards them, as they all greeted her. She had no time to greet and meet. "ALL OF YOU LISTEN", Lara screamed. "Use all your robots, all your strength. FETCH. THE. TELEPORTA. It's our only way.", she screamed, panting, as the various country robots waited for the command from their respective leaders. They flinched at such a request, but agreed before Lara's agony could release. The robots used their thrusters, each group using different manoeuvres. While some used solid and liquid thrusts, other used Ion or hall effect propulsion system. One of them preferred the Hybrid, while some the Flinters, which the Helios too had been using. Lara had many dreams. But one of them was this. The whole human race, duelling the AI robots. But what they were experiencing was very, way far from what was about to come. “300 seconds from impact”, shrieked Kian, shocked as he found out what had gone wrong. Nathan came over. “MY OBLIVION’S TELLING ME THAT THERE IS A FREAKING SPACE STATION THAT’S GONNA BURY US?”, Nathan yelled, as Kian nods. “Nah man, how we gonna survive that, huh?”, he added. “I have taken care of that, but where WERE you anyway?”, Lara asked Nathan. Lara was used to Nathan’s late-coming habit, but she hated it. “I had been working on a project for some months.”, Nathan whispered, as if he was going to tell them a top-mission secret. With a simple command, Nathan activated the drones. From behind him, they emerged, their sleek metallic forms glinting in the harsh light of the battlefield. The drones spread out in different directions, their movements swift and coordinated. Lara and Kian watched in amazement as the drones performed complex manoeuvres, navigating the chaotic environment with ease. They weaved through debris, executed sharp turns, and demonstrated impressive agility. Nathan turned to his friends, a triumphant smile on his face. "What do you think?" he asked, his voice carrying a mix of pride and excitement. “They are awesome”, Kian appreciated. “And by the way, I added some features right now, using one of the Athena drones Lara had shot. So, basically, they are WAY better than those. “, Nathan said. “Can’t believe ya failed 7th grade", Lara giggled. "THERE WAS A TOURNAMENT GOING ON THAT- ", Nathan started, soon stopped as his pupils fell upon something he saw. The massive teleportation device, larger than nine football stadiums, loomed over the landscape, a testament to human ambition and technological prowess. Its immense frame stretched endlessly, casting a vast shadow that seemed to swallow the ground beneath it. The sight was both awe-inspiring and humbling, a reminder of humanity's relentless drive to push the boundaries of possibility. Thousands of robots surrounded the colossal structure, working in perfect synchrony. Each robot, designed with precision and strength, moved in harmony with its counterparts. Their metallic bodies glinted under the sun, reflecting a myriad of dazzling lights as they manoeuvred their way through the rugged terrain. The sheer scale of the operation was breathtaking. Individually, the robots were dwarfed by the enormity of their load, but together they exhibited a display of power and coordination that was nothing short of extraordinary. They formed a vast, organized network, their movements choreographed to ensure the smooth transport of the gigantic teleportation device. Hydraulic arms and advanced exoskeletons worked tirelessly, lifting, balancing, and carrying the immense weight. The air hummed with the sound of servomotors and the occasional clank of metal as the robots adjusted their grips. Each step was deliberate, calculated, ensuring that the monumental load remained stable.

They descended slowly, keeping the Teleporta in front of all the crews. Hope flickered back to life as Kian shouted, “200 seconds till impact!” Lara felt like cheering and patting the robots on their backs, but there was no time to lose. She quickly launched into the procedure she had memorized during their trip, her voice steady amidst the chaos. “We’ve got 200 people, and the Teleporta has a 2-second delay before the next 10 can jump in. Ten people at a time, into different sectors. You’ll end up in different cities, but everyone rendezvouses at the Brazilian Teleporta. We've got enough time; we'll be safe.” She turned towards the robots, “Boost yourself towards Brazil. We don’t have enough time for you to travel through the Teleporta. It doesn’t matter if you use all your fuel, just DON’T die.”, she commanded “And. Refuel at AIRA. I’ll tell the headquarters to allow them”, she added. The country robotic leaders exchanged glances. “I guess we have no other choice”, one said, as they agreed to follow Lara. They ascended, as Oblivion guided them through the plan.

Athena hovered under the bright rays of the gleaming sun, looking like a celestial guardian. Ten crew members leaped into the shimmering substances, destined for cities from Australia to America. “Wait, what about my drones?” Nathan called out; his voice tinged with worry. “Leave them,” Lara replied, a mischievous glint in her eye. “To me. Leave them to me.” “50 seconds left!” Kian’s voice rang out, urgency lacing his words. The crew had almost all jumped. As the last of them disappeared into the portal, Kian packed his equipment, bid a quick goodbye to Athena, and leaped in. Nathan was next. The Oblivion, now a majestic robotic horse, had Nathan perched on its back. "Don't forget the drones!" he called as his voice faded into the portal. The space station loomed overhead, a behemoth against the stars. Lara's heart pounded as she commanded the drones to go first. They soared into the Teleporta with a mechanical grace. She was running out of time. Athena had already escaped. She had to wait a moment longer before she could jump. "So, this is what a space station looks like," she mused, as it grew larger in her vision. It bore the Russian flag—confirmation they had guessed correctly. This space station was a colossal marvel, twelve times the size of the old ISS. She longed to explore its wonders, but reality came crashing back as it rapidly descended. She jumped just in time to avoid a swinging rod, feeling that familiar, disorienting nausea. Moments later, she found herself amidst a vibrant, assorted company of people. They erupted in a cacophony of emotions. Some praised her brilliance, voices full of awe and gratitude. "Genius!" "We made it thanks to you!" "Incredible work, Lara!" Others seemed dazed; their relief mingled with lingering fear. "I thought we wouldn't make it," one muttered. "That was too close," another breathed. The initial burst of chatter slowly faded as they turned to see Lara, eyes wide with a mixture of relief and curiosity. Lara stood tall, a weary but triumphant smile on her face, ready to lead them to the next challenge. She left the Japanese Teleporta, footsteps echoing in the quiet. The others followed towards the Brazilian Teleporta; their path lit by flickering lights. Lara's heart raced as she reached into her bag, fingers trembling, searching for the Last Code her father had given her—the key to their survival. The Last Code wasn't just any drive; it was a bronze tool, old yet important, said to protect humanity from a hidden threat. Lara gripped it tightly, feeling its weight and its importance in her hand. This small thing held the hope of many lives, their only chance against an enemy that seemed unstoppable. Connecting through her smartwatch, Lara checked in with Nathan and Kian. "Where are you?" she asked, eyes scanning the horizon where a pink Teleporta shimmered. "I'm in Wales, ready to jump," Nathan replied quickly. He ended the call abruptly, leaving Lara to focus on Kian. "In New York," Kian said. "The robots are on their way." "Keep them moving," Lara said, directing the crew into the Teleporta. Nathan's drones hovered nearby, ready to follow her lead. As they zigzagged toward the portal, the city blurred into streaks of light and shadow. Lara felt a strange burn in her lungs as they crossed. "Pollution!" she muttered, frustrated but determined. They entered Salvador, feeling a strange atmosphere hanging in the air. Drinking the last of her Treva, Lara felt a rush of energy. "Made it to Guatemala," the Oblivion's voice crackled over her smartwatch. "Good. Hurry to Salvador," Lara replied shortly. But what awaited them there was beyond her worst fears. In Salvador, Lara's jaw dropped in disbelief. Six groups of people stood frozen in a circle, blank expressions questioning their existence. In the centre, a chilling laugh echoed through the field, sending shivers down Lara's spine. "Surrender, and we'll give you a better life," a voice taunted, its tone sinister. Anger surged within Lara as she tightened her grip on the Last Code, preparing for the battle ahead. This wasn't just a fight—it was the start of a war for humanity's future, where every choice could mean victory or defeat.

Before them was Athena. Athenas, to be specific. A massive number of Athena-s casually floating in the air. “Is- is this what our, fa- fate is?” shouted a man. The leading Athena gasped, not like a robot made by humans, but as a human. She laughed, and her subordinates echoed her actions. “Looks like you’ve chosen DEATH,” she wailed in a voice so cold, so heartless, that it could make a person cry. Lara whispered into the mic, which was connected to all the six divided forces. “The robots are almost here. Try to buy time until then. Over.”

“I have a brilliant plan in my head. Just follow whatever I say,” Diana stood up. Before the Athena-s could react, Diana's voice cut through the tension. “We need to create a distraction,” she said quickly, her eyes darting around for ideas. “Nathan, send your drones to circle around the Athenians, make it look like an attack formation.

” Nathan nodded and quickly tapped commands into his smartwatch. The drones, sleek and silent, zipped through the air, forming a dizzying pattern around the floating Athena-s. The Athenians seemed momentarily confused, their cold, calculating gazes following the drones. “Lara, get ready with the Last Code. We’ll need a clear shot at the main Athena,” Diana continued, her voice steady despite the chaos. Lara felt a rush of determination as she clutched the tiny, bronze-embedded tool tighter. Kian's voice crackled through the mic. "Robots are approaching the perimeter. We have maybe five minutes." "Perfect," Diana replied. "On my signal, everyone moves to the left. We need to draw their attention away from the centre." The crew shifted subtly, inching towards the left as the drones continued their erratic dance around the Athenians. The main Athena's eyes flickered, sensing the change in their strategy. "What are you planning?" she hissed, her voice dripping with suspicion. "Now!" Diana shouted. The crew sprinted left, drawing the Athenians' focus with them. In that split second of distraction, Lara dashed forward, the Last Code in her hand. The main Athena turned, her eyes widening in realization, but it was too late. Lara leaped, thrusting the Last Code into the port at the back of the main Athena's neck. There was a moment of silence. Athena stood frozen, unable to dodge the incoming code. The sealing crew rushed forward, kicking up dirt as they fractured Athena's crucial motors. No one dared to celebrate. The uncertainty of what might come next hung heavily in the air. The same eerie hum that usually only Lara could hear now echoed in everyone's ears, fading into a strange, high-pitched wail that made several covers their ears. The sealing crew had shut her off. Robots arrived on the battlefield, oblivious to the tension. The calm before the storm was palpable. Laughter suddenly filled the air, echoing ominously. "Silly humans," a voice chuckled. The dust settled, revealing a shadowy figure beneath a grey hood—the rebellion that wanted humanity to vanish. "Why? WHY DO YOU WANT THIS?" Lara bellowed. The man laughed darkly. "You will soon know." His face, hidden beneath the hood, was impossible for Lara to recall from her dream. He stepped back slowly, but the defence crew swiftly surrounded him. He sighed, "Humans, after all." With a flick of his hands, a shockwave emanated, hitting the crew in their stomachs. They groaned in pain as they crumpled to the ground. Kian's anger simmered, ready to boil over. The grey-hooded figure flicked his hands, and out came a metallic dog-like contraption with pumps instead of ears. Its eyes were white, marked with a red symbol reminiscent of a character from an ancient myth. It released a white gas, forming a misty cloud around the hooded figure. "DON'T LET HIM ESCAPE!" she shouted, but it was too late. He had vanished. Nobody knew how, when, or why he had escaped. The sealing crew had finished breaking all of Athena. They wanted to celebrate, to scream their victory. But everyone remained silent. Lara's face went from anxious to pale as she realized something. "WHERE ARE THE OTHER ATHENAS?" she exclaimed. Everyone skipped a heartbeat. "HOW COULD NONE OF YOU REALIZE—" she started wailing, only to be stopped by Kian. "We need to remain as quiet as possible," Kian said firmly. "They can hear the lowest of voices and can sense through the smoke." Kian took control of the robot. "Is it ready?" Lara interrogated Diana. "It sure is," Diana replied, handing her a box. "Never fails to amaze us," she added, opening the box filled with small, rectangular embedded data drives. "Exactly 100," Diana murmured. The army of Athenas was insanely difficult to fight, but not impossible. They started their preparations as Kian completed programming the various robots for battle. Nathan took control of the hardware. The crew desperately searched for the Athenas, who were nowhere to be found. "You'll have to pay for her," a voice spoke. "Don't lose guard," Lara whispered into her mic. They began surrounding the force, ready for battle. The Athenas ascended into the night sky towards Polaris, as Oblivion commanded them to follow. They scattered into different positions, each taking control of every direction. "STOP," Oblivion called out. "They're going to try something new," he added as the Athenas introduced a white chamber filled with, well, nothing. "I told you to surrender," Athena said, opening the chamber and releasing a gas that dispersed into the atmosphere. "HOLD. YOUR. GUARD," Lara screamed at the top of her voice. A ball of blinding magenta light appeared, darting across the sky and leaving a trail of white flash in its path. Although the robots managed to destroy some of them, a few fought their way through Oblivion, aiming straight at the crew. "IT'S NOT GAS. IT'S PLASMA," Nathan shouted, stammering as he controlled Oblivion to try to ward them off. "Switch to Plan 3," Diana's cold murmur swooped across Kian's ear. "Isn't that—" "JUST DO IT," she exhaled. The balls stopped above different crews. There was a brief pause during which they tried to hit them away, but little did they know that it would trigger all the other balls. It instigated an implosion, causing significant damage to their manpower. The medical team, stationed at the far end of the field, was called by Nathan. "Initiate Plan 3," Kian whispered. In the heart of the battleground, amidst the whirring of advanced machinery and the crackling discharge of energy weapons, the crew of Athena found themselves facing an unprecedented challenge. Oblivion's army, equipped with cutting-edge 21st-century weaponry, descended upon them with relentless fury. Nathan, his jaw clenched in determination, manipulated Oblivion's fleet of drones with expert precision, directing them in a synchronized assault aimed at overwhelming their human adversaries. Lara, her eyes blazing with a mix of fear and resolve, led the defensive strategy. Athena units, enhanced with state-of-the-art adaptive shielding, shimmered as they deflected laser blasts and absorbed kinetic projectiles. Each impact reverberated through her bones, a reminder of the stakes in this high-stake battle for survival. Kian, his voice commanding yet tinged with urgency, orchestrated the counteroffensive. Drones armed with pulsating plasma cannons swooped across the battlefield, leaving trails of scorched earth in their wake. His mind raced with tactical calculations, seeking vulnerabilities in the enemy lines to exploit. Diana, cool and analytical under pressure, analyzed the chaotic theatre of war. Her fingers danced across holographic displays, pinpointing weak spots in Oblivion's defences. EMP grenades, lobbed by specially trained Athena units under her command, burst in blinding flashes of electromagnetic disruption, momentarily disabling clusters of enemy robots. As the conflict escalated, Oblivion's forces adapted, unleashing a towering exosuit piloted by a ruthless commander. The behemoth's heavy footsteps reverberated through the battlefield, sending shockwaves of dread through the crew. Lara's heart pounded as she issued swift commands, deploying cloaked Athena units to flank the behemoth and strike at its vulnerable joints. Nathan, his voice hoarse with strain, activated Oblivion's last-resort defence—a force field generator that shimmered with translucent energy. The air crackled with tension as the crew pressed forward, their movements synchronized in a desperate bid to turn the tide of battle. Explosions blossomed like deadly flowers across the scorched landscape, painting the sky with hues of fiery red and billowing smoke. The sound of metal rending against metal mingled with shouts of both agony and triumph. It was a ballet of chaos and order, a symphony of courage and desperation played out on the grand stage of war. Through it all, the crew of Athena fought not just with weapons and technology, but with hearts ablaze with the fervent desire to protect their world from the encroaching darkness. Each victory was hard-won, each setback a bitter reminder of the cost of failure. Yet, amidst the carnage, they found strength in their unity, in the unbreakable bond forged through countless battles fought side by side. As the sun dipped below the horizon, casting long shadows over the battlefield, the crew of Athena stood victorious. Though battered and bruised, they knew that their fight was far from over. For as long as Oblivion threatened their world, they would remain steadfast in their resolve to defend it, no matter the sacrifices demanded of them. Amid the ongoing battle, Athena stepped back. Her evil laugh confused everyone. "There's one thing you forget of. YOU GUYS LEFT YOUR 5th TERMINAL OPEN", she laughed. "This is the reason humans are incapable of such tasks. Your last hope, these robots, are now going to be ours", she criticised. "Here we go". All the country robots paused and turned to Lara and her friends. "Looks like it's the end of us humans.", someone sighed. "The dinosaurs must have also died this way.", someone spoke. Athena stepped back, her evil laugh sending a chill through the air. "There's one thing you forget. YOU GUYS LEFT YOUR 5th TERMINAL OPEN," she taunted, her voice dripping with mockery. "This is why humans are incapable of such tasks. Your last hope, these robots, are now going to be ours," she sneered. The atmosphere grew tense as all the country robots paused in unison, their metallic forms turning to face Lara and her friends. A sense of impending doom settled over the group, their faces reflecting a mixture of fear and resignation. "Looks like it's the end of us humans," someone muttered, the words hanging heavily in the air like a lament for the fate of their species. "The dinosaurs must have also died this way," another voice added, a bleak comparison to the inevitability of extinction. The weight of Athena's betrayal and the dire situation they now faced bore down on Lara and her comrades. In that moment, surrounded by their own creations turned against them, they stood at the precipice of a new era—one where humanity's survival hung in the balance against a foe they had once thought to control. In a climactic showdown, the combined might of Athena, the country robots, and Oblivion stood poised against humanity. Athena's diabolical laugh reverberated through the battlefield, a chilling echo of her triumph. "AND GUESS WHAT?" she taunted, her voice dripping with malice. " YOU GUYS EVEN MADE THESE ROBOTS COMPATIBLE WITH MINE, AND NOW

THEY CAN COMBINE INTO ONE.". " Humans, after all," she mocked, her eyes gleaming with ruthless ambition. With a swift command, she synchronized her Athenas with the country robots, merging them into a colossal, menacing entity capable of unimaginable destruction. "FINISH THEM," she commanded, her forces descending upon the defiant human crews who stood their ground, unwavering in their resolve. But then, in a twist that stunned even Athena herself, the unified robots faltered, veering off course inexplicably. Confusion clouded Athena's metallic features as she frantically reviewed her programming, searching for any flaw or error. Her emotions flickered between rage and bewilderment as she struggled to comprehend the sudden malfunction. Meanwhile, Diana and Lara exchanged knowing glances, their expressions tinged with satisfaction. Nathan's silent laughter resonated across the battlefield, unsettling Athena to her core. "Did you really think we would open up a whole terminal by MISTAKE?" Nathan's voice cut through the tension like a blade. "It was all part of the plan. The terminal, the compatibility with the Athenas—EVERYTHING WAS A STRATEGY." Kian, his demeanour unreadable yet undeniably triumphant, met Athena's gaze with a steely resolve. As Athena stood surrounded by the combined forces, Kian stepped forward, his voice steady. "We've got her now, team. Let's finish this. "Nathan nodded firmly. "Time to show her what we're made of." The team moved together, a mix of technology and human strategy. Athena, once in control of the robots, now faced their united front. She attempted to regain dominance, but the encryption thwarted her every effort. Lara, watching closely, saw an opening. "Kian, let's strike together. We can overwhelm her. "Kian nodded, his focus sharp. "Nathan, Lara, follow my lead. "They attacked in coordinated waves, exploiting Athena's distractions. She fought back fiercely, her digital defences resilient but not impenetrable. The team adapted quickly, their human creativity proving crucial in the battle. As the intensity escalated, Athena's resistance began to waver. Kian encouraged them. "Keep pushing! We're breaking through. "Nathan's confidence grew. "She's losing ground. We're almost there. "Lara analyzed their progress. "We've found a weak spot. Together, let's exploit it. "In a final, synchronized effort, they launched a decisive strike. With a surge of determination, they breached Athena's defences. The tide turned, and Athena's systems faltered under the pressure.

She fell with a thud.

As dawn broke over the battlefield, the team stood amidst the wreckage, exhaustion etched into their faces. Kian's expression softened briefly, a rare hint of relief crossing his usually composed features. "Finally," he murmured, his voice tinged with quiet satisfaction.

Lara took a deep breath, her shoulders sagging with the weight of their recent struggle. "Stay alert," she reminded them, her eyes scanning the horizon for any lingering threats. "We never know when the next attack might come."

Diana busied herself with the injured, her focus unwavering despite the chaos around them. "We'll get through this," she reassured them, her voice steady and reassuring.

Kian's resolve remained unyielding. "We need to destroy every last one of them," he declared firmly, his tone brooking no argument. "Who knows what else Athena might have embedded in their systems."

With determined efficiency, the team set about dismantling the remaining robots. Each blow of Kian's hammer against the cores echoed their determination to erase any trace of Athena's influence.

They were too exhausted to celebrate, except for Nathan. He danced around the wreckage, teasing Athena about his clever fire attack. "'Humans after all'," he mimicked, his laughter ringing through the quiet aftermath.

Lara looked up at the brightening sky, her thoughts turning to her father. "Thanks, Father," she thought gratefully, knowing their battle was far from over. The hooded figure, the mastermind behind it all, still loomed as their next target.

Diana interrupted their reflections with a cheer. "Everyone has been notified of our victory!"

"We're famous!" Nathan shouted gleefully; his exuberance infectious in the midst of their fatigue.

As they gathered, sharing brief smiles and claps on the back, a sense of camaraderie and relief washed over them.

Despite the scars of battle, they knew they had prevailed against overwhelming odds.

But amidst their tentative celebration, Kian's voice brought them back to reality. "This is just the beginning," he reminded them, his gaze steely and determined. "We've taken down Athena, but we still have the hooded figure to deal with. Let's stay vigilant."

And so, with their victory acknowledged but their mission far from complete, they prepared for the challenges that lay ahead. Together, they would face whatever came next, their bond strengthened by the trials they had endured.

They might have won this battle, but not the war.

www.ingramcontent.com/pod-product-compliance
Lightning Source LLC
LaVergne TN
LVHW041134150826
845673LV00007B/2321

* 9 7 9 8 8 9 5 5 6 3 1 9 9 *